Thomas
AND THE DINOSAUR

by Christopher Awdry

illustrated by Ken Stott

Heinemann · London

First published in Great Britain 1992 by
William Heinemann Ltd
an imprint of Reed Children's Books
Michelin House, 81 Fulham Road, London SW3 6RB
and Auckland, Melbourne, Singapore and Toronto

Reprinted 1992, 1993 (twice), 1994

ISBN 0 434 96068 3

A CIP catalogue record for this book is available
at the British Library.

Printed in Great Britain by
Cambus Litho Limited, East Kilbride

"I saw a dragon today," Percy said in the shed one day.
"Dragons breathe fire and eat engines."

Next day Thomas had just left the junction with Annie and Clarabel when he saw an enormous animal standing beside the line.

"That must be Percy's dragon," he thought, "but it's not breathing fire." Thomas decided that the dragon must be asleep.

At the top station they were met by the Fat Controller.
"There is an emergency, Thomas," he said.

"I would like you to take a flat truck to the junction
for a special train."

At the junction a signalman told Thomas where to take
the flat truck.
"But that's where the dragon is," said Thomas anxiously.

The signalman laughed. "Don't worry, Thomas," he said.
"It won't eat you. It's only a model dinosaur. It looks real,
but it's just made of wood and plaster."

"What's a dinosaur?" asked Thomas.
"It's a prehistoric animal which lived millions of years ago,"
  explained his driver.

"Oh, that's all right then," said Thomas. "Percy thought it was a fire-breathing dragon which ate engines."

His driver laughed. "It's an exhibit for a new show near the top station," he said. "The lorry carrying it broke down, so we've got to take it instead."

The workmen fastened the hook to the chains round the dinosaur. Then, at a signal, Harold lifted the model very carefully.

Harold carried the dinosaur over to Thomas's waiting truck. Then, very gently he lowered it, and the workmen made sure it would not slip during the journey.

Then Thomas set off. The dinosaur was very light, so he had an easy run. Children ran to wave as he passed by with his unusual load.

At the middle station, they met Percy. He looked
frightened when he saw what Thomas was carrying.

"One, two, three, lift," ordered the Fat Controller.
Carefully the breakdown crane lifted the model dinosaur
over the fence into the nearby gardens.

Soon it was safely on the exhibition site with the other dinosaurs.

Now everything was ready for the grand opening.

Three cheers for Thomas and all the dinosaurs!